Ice Queen's Daddy

Roberta Blackmore

Contents

Summary

Avery Blanc is known as the "Ice Queen" of the corporate world because she is icy, formidable, and accurate. Her life isn't as flawless as it looks, however, and when she falls pregnant after an unintentional one-night encounter, she's resolved to keep the child. In order to appease her family, she has her attractive secretary act as the father of the child and her fiancé. In reality, Tristan Hayes is the phoney baby daddy and fiancée of his employer, despite having applied for a job as a secretary. As he gets to know Avery more, he comes to fall for her, but the mysteries surrounding his actual identity threaten to destroy all they've built together.

Chapter 1 - A Night To Remember

Egotistical jerk who thinks only about himself.The offer was promptly discarded by Avery Blanc, who returned her focus to her job.But concentration was elusive.Douglas Marsh has built a career on manipulating others for his own ends. When it came to this, she was the undisputed expert.For all she knew, the offer was his last-ditch effort to get her worked up. To keep with tradition.Given how things had concluded between them, it was predictable that he would do something like that.He should have anticipated that, given how things ended between them, she would sooner ingest a gallon of jet fuel than show up to his wedding.She straightened her back and jutted her chin out as she stared intently at her laptop. There was no need for the CEO of one of New York's most successful corporations to take it out on her ex, who was a worthless jerk.Avery heard a soft tap on the door and sprang to attention.As Tristan smiled half-heartedly and brought in some presents, he introduced himself.As he set down the coffee and chocolate chip muffin, she bit back her wrath.She replied, "Thanks," but her mouth was sealed.There was no need to disturb her solitude at the moment. However, her secretary behaved as if she were unaware of this, as is her custom.He sat down at her desk, staring absently into her trash can.As in, "Is everything all right?"A question mark appeared in his eyes. You're a little bit spacey, it seems.A sigh escaped the plush leather as she relaxed back in her seat. She crossed her arms across her chest and looked at him with a puzzled expression.She saw his conscious attempt to prevent his gaze from straying to her legs. He was making a concerted effort to avoid accidentally catching the hem of her expensive skirt as it rode up her thighs.She couldn't possibly say she didn't like the way she made guys feel.You're different, you have to realise that."As he moved, he felt a little out of place. How can you explain that? ""You simply seem to have a sixth sense about my requirements."A grin of accomplishment appeared on his face, and she gazed in awe. The sight of it caused a tightening in her chest.Except now, she said, her voice steely and icy.His grin vanished in an instant."I didn't ask for this," she said dismissively, waving her hand at the muffin sitting on her desk. You shouldn't have knocked on my door since it's closed."I'm sorry, I just-"I didn't need your apology, either," she added abruptly.The words she said to him were like an icicle that sank straight into his soul. Instead of feeling down, Avery was able to find some solace.Her gut knot loosed at the sight of his tormented countenance. The tension that hadn't been released since she'd accepted that ill-advised invitation.I apologise, Miss Blanc. Sorry if I offended you.Get out, she glared at him firmly.As he got up from her desk, Tristan sighed and looked defeated. He continued on until he was standing in front of her office door, at which point he turned around.Please tell me if there's anything more I can get you." he inquired, his voice cracking under the exertion of keeping his composure.Okay, screw him. To her, it didn't matter how he was feeling at the moment. Everything that happened was his fault since he forced his way in.Cancel my 4:00," she replied, turning away from the pitiful figure he had made in her doorway. "And please, for the love of God, ignore any calls."The sound of the door shutting behind him was the cue she needed to take a deep breath, and she did so with trepidation.Her father handed her the reins at Blanc Holdings, but he didn't tell her about the heavy armour she'd need to wear.Her PC emitted a faint ding. It's a brand fresh email. Her four o'clock email with the subject line "You're cancelling again?" ’"I need to get out of here," she said, edging away from her desk and gathering her belongings.***Amnesia was an exclusive sex club frequented by Hollywood's A-list. There were stringent regulations in place to limit interaction between the club's privileged clientele and others of similar social standing.It's an exclusive club, and nobody else is welcome.Additionally, they were required to wear masks at all times, making them completely unidentifiable to everyone, even each other.Only those who have been invited are allowed in. Customers could do whatever the heck they wanted, with anybody they wanted, without worrying about the following day's tabloids.Avery ordered a "dirty martini" from the bartender and sat down. Furthermore, please continue sending them.Avery drank her first martini in an attempt to dull her irritation, but it had the opposite effect. She chugged another, and her impatience grew.The bartender leaned forward across the counter and said, "Let me guess." "There is something you need to put out of your mind.""I can't believe his cockiness, for the life of me!" I mean, here I am, trying to put this guy out of my mind for the last five years, and he invites me to his wedding! Know how frustrating that is? ”Avery signalled the bartender that her glass was empty, and she promptly received a new one.Does it make you want him back, or what?”She gulped the drink and glared at the bartender, saying, "God no, the emotional trauma he did me was enough to last me a lifetime." It's been five years since the day he crushed my hopes and ambitions, and it seems he still can't let go.It seems you can't let go either," the bartender stated as he set down the refill.She lowered her head, and moved her drink around in her palms. Incredulous, she told the bartender her story as if she were an alcoholic. However, I did get some relief from it.I devoted the greater part of my life to that one person. I had feelings for him for a long time, but he finally drove me away. Then I decided to just leave. Honestly, I didn't even think about turning around.Even if you deny it, what he did to you stings even though it was difficult for you. Do you mind if I offered some suggestions? ”I mean, why the heck not?", she asked, raising her glass before chugging it dry.You shouldn't allow a guy like him to have power over your life or your emotions because you are still young and you are wonderfully gorgeous. He seemed to have been doing so for much longer than was acceptable. Don't dwell on the past, and start living in the present. After all, it's your only option.The logic in his remarks let her harden her heart again.She held out her freshly filled glass and said, "Let me buy you a drink."The bartender also mixed a drink for himself and displayed it.She clinked her glass with his and stated, "With you as my witness, I pledge that I will never allow Douglas Marsh put me in such a position again."The bartender said, "That's the spirit," as the patrons drank their beverages.While she waited for her drink, she looked around the club. There was cash wherever you looked. Expensive brands writhed on the dance floor to the beat of generic deep funk.Don't serve me a Martini just yet. She finally voiced her impatience, "I want to dance."She rose to her feet and began winding her way among the people. She was brimming with self-assurance and pride. No one could ever take away from her the freedom to be herself.She felt the pulse pulsate through her body, beginning at the base of her neck and ending somewhere in her upper chest. She reached up and slid her hands up her thighs, her middle finger hovering just over her breasts, before reaching up and burying it in her hair.Not too long passed before she became aware that she was being observed. Yes, she had drawn attention to herself. Obviously, everyone wants to.However, this was not the case. A lot of thought had gone into this, and it showed.She swivelled gently on the dance floor, her gaze sweeping the throng until it settled on a single individual. Someone was hiding in the shadows, sitting in his seat all by himself and shamelessly monitoring her the whole time.She was drawn to him by the aura of mystery and gloom that surrounds him. The mystery captivated her, and she want to delve into its underbelly. He took a forward lean, clearly pleased with what he saw, and she couldn't help but give in.Avery kept up her sultry dance, but this time she was performing for him alone. She maintained steady eye contact with the unknown man as he moved his hands freely over her body.The woman accepted his twisted invitation to join him at his table. Her heart pounded as she walked toward him.His hazel eyes shone through the fine jewel-encrusted craftsmanship of his matte black mask, even in the pitch darkness. His caramel hair was slicked back nicely, and his jawline was sharp enough to chop through a brick.Avery saw the delectable way his black Armani suit clung to his muscular physique and commented, "You seem to appreciate what you see."His brow furrowed as he tapped the unoccupied seat next to him. Is there any stunning woman that would want to come have a drink with me? ”A pool of heat formed between her legs as the low rumble of his voice reverberated through her bones.It's hard to think that a mysterious, gorgeous guy like yourself doesn't already had company," Avery stated as she sat down next to him.When there's a chance I might meet someone as interesting as you, why would I bother bringing anyone else?He moved very close to her and said, ".Avery stroked his bare chest and added, "That type of nice words will go you a long way."Just tell me what you need.While his hands lingered on her thigh, he asked.Avery had never had such instant chemistry with another person, yet there was something about the unknown guy that she couldn't deny. She wasn't looking to hook up with anybody, but he was something else entirely. It was as if he had some kind of enchantment that caused her to forget the purpose of her visit, and she wished that effect might stay forever.She muttered, "I'll take another martini," and stepped in for a closer look.He threw his arm around her and said, "You are stunningly lovely."She felt instantly at ease from the warmth coming off of him. It was like balm to her troubled spirit. She became so engrossed in the moment that she gave in to her overwhelming want to touch him.His presence was just what she needed at this time. The only way she could forget about her problems was to be with him. He may be able to help her put the past in the past.She remarked as she slid her fingers up his leg, "Such a charmer. A female would be silly to say no. ”He took her hand and held it to his massive, fully erect shaft without saying a word or hesitating. Avery contemplated the sensation of carrying him inside her and bit her lower lip.The moment she began to touch him, he let out a deep sigh.His voice shook as he said, "Damn, that feels amazing."The way his words aroused her ardour was wonderful, and she want more. Why don't you kiss me if it's so pleasurable?" ”She pressed her lips to his and forcefully demanded what she wanted. His sexual energy jolted through her in waves, awakening all of her nerve ends.The intensity of their kiss grew rapidly. It seemed to him like he could swallow her whole right then.She gladly gave in to his advances.

All she wanted was to lose herself in his arms. To be captured by a rough and macho guy who would make her submit.His fingers moved slowly up her bare thigh and nestled between her legs. Jesus, he breathed out weakly, was his only response. You're so fucking wet that it hurts me.Do you find that appealing?"The girl whispered sweet nothings in his ear.Between her smooth lips, his fingers stroked rapidly and firmly. She locked her thighs firmly around his fingers to increase the pressure, waves of ecstasy shooting through her body.Accept it. Saying, "Take my cock," he dipped his head to nibble at the area below her ear. The phrase "I want to feel your warm hand around it" comes to mind.There was no need to tell her again. After Avery undid his trousers, she wrapped her slim fingers around his aching cock.As she stroked him forcefully, moving her thumb up to touch his exposed tip, a gasp echoed from the back of his throat. The man was drenched.To which the question, "Is that for me?" she retreated to meet his gaze.In response to his "fuck yes," he moaningly kissed his way down her neck. "God... Until now, no one had ever hit me that hard.He straddled her, hands firmly placed on her hips, the tip of his cock teasingly beckoning her closer.Her hands shook as she pushed the hem of her dress up higher than her derriere. She sank herself onto the dashing stranger, holding her breath the whole while.Until she was wide out, she gazed at the length of his cock, and then their pubic bones kissed in the most tantalising manner imaginable. For a brief while, she was completely absorbed by him, just as she had hoped, and she forgot about Douglas entirely. She was completely focused on the mysterious man in the dark who was nestled between her legs.His hands wandered all over her, setting off a wave of chills that swept through her. He moaned as he grasped her tight arse and they shifted positions.He pressed his breath against her ear as he drove farther into her, thinking to himself, "You're the sort of lady every man dreams of."Avery paused for a moment after closing her eyes and uttering a loud gasp. She was aware that every man had fantasised about her, but she just couldn't seem to attract "the one." She needed someone who would appreciate her for more than just her wealth.He would be the type of guy who would give his all to her without asking for anything in return. The one who could return her affections in kind. Since she was well aware that such a man did not exist, the very concept of him caused her irritation.She rocked her hips and said, "I don't give a damn about what every man wants." "Right now, nothing matters except losing myself in this moment with you."Then, his shaft throbbed against her walls as he emptied her entirely. She had to be cautious since she didn't want it to stop too soon.Her actions were planned out yet sluggish. Extraction of pure enjoyment from every possible source.He responded, "Let me do the fucking," and he fucked her hair as he brought her face close to his.She took a deep, nervous breath in.

“Yes.”Before she could react, he leaped up and flipped the table behind her, sending it squeaking across the floor.She was placed on the seat by strong hands, kneeling, with her torso slung over the backrest.This change in dynamic was thrilling, and it added fire to her already blazing desire. It was just what she was searching for. The freedom to relax the strict discipline she felt compelled to maintain daily.Even if it was just some stranger fucking her at a club, she just needed someone else to take care of things for a minute. Even if it lasted for just a short while.She gasped, "Oh God, yeah."As he rear-ended her, she saw stars fly past her headlights. Following that, he repeated the action. Also, once more.She bit down on her palm to suppress sobs of sheer bliss that were filling her to bursting.Her legs started to shake and juices were dripping down them. Her clit began to pulse as arousal coiled itself around her.With a mumbled "Oh God," she exclaimed her shock. Keep going.A hand stretched around and, with two fingers, he caressed her clit as if reading it like a book. Immediately, the tension that had been accumulating there began to release.However, he never slowed his forward momentum. As if his life depended on it, he recklessly ploughed into her.He murmured as he sank his fangs into her shoulder, "I'm going to make you cum so fucking hard."She pressed her arched back into him and swung her arm back to around his neck.Deeper. She required him to probe further. I decided to take her up on her offer of everything.As she wailed, he pressed on her more more. They had both reached the point of no return and were continuing on anyway.Between his finely operated fingers, he wedged himself between her knees, while the other hand gripped her hip.He stood up and slapped her ass hard with one hand while pushing her face into the booth's plush leather with the other.His smack hurt like hell, sending electric shocks right to her swollen clit. Her defences hardened around his scrotum, and she felt her life force rapidly draining away.God, she wanted it. He needed to push her over so she could lose herself in the moment. Her body craved for the sensation, something she hadn't had in a long time.It echoed in the silence of the club as he hit her again.Her trembling legs were on the verge of giving out from beneath her.Do you like that kind of thing?And then he smacked her again, driving his whole body into her, this time moving much more quickly.She felt his pantyhose get hot and his breath rush in. She also sensed his proximity to her.She leaned back and whispered, "Finish me" as she reached up and slid her fingers through his thick, dark hair. "God, I want you to kill me so badly."Embraced in the dark, their sweaty bodies clung to one another as they waited for that sweet release to overpower them.He snatched her ear off. He sighed and squeezed her clit between his fingers, saying, "Oh God, I'm cumming."As the waves of her climax smashed through her, Avery bit her lip but couldn't stifle the strangled howl that tore from her throat.The tension was now gone, and he was able to unleash his entire sexual fury on her. He let go of her clit and switched to quick stroking so she could ride it out."Oh. Fuck. Ahhhhh! "The stranger jerked and trembled his way to climax, ramming into her until every last drop of him was spent.Avery felt as though she'd never regain the full use of her legs as she shakily returned to a seated position, trying to catch her breath. After zipping up his trousers, he sat down next to her, and she observed.Running a timid finger up her moist thigh, he gathered her secretions and, locking his gaze with hers, drew the flavour of her into his lips.Even though she was absolutely drained, she felt fantastic. Her worries were gone, and she couldn't remember what had been bothering her before.As her lungs struggled to take in breath again, she peered up into his hypnotic eyes. She was in a state of pure bliss, yet she still saw the fleeting expression in those hazel eyes.It's like, "Do- do I know you?Avery said in a hushed voice.

Chapter 2 - An Unexpected Pregnancy

Tristan saw Avery go back to her office and realised she seemed preoccupied. He thought it would be wise to attempt to distract her from her worries, so he made another order at her favourite coffee shop.While she was on the phone, he studied her from his reclined position. He didn't feel awful about eavesdropping since her door was open.The caller said, "Hey, Mom, could you grab Dad and make this a conference call? 'I have to tell you both something,' Avery said.Naturally, sweetie. Maybe a video chat would be better? Mrs. Blanc said, "We haven't seen you in ages.Instead, "Let me just grab Dad, and I'll-""You're constantly working," her mother said. We can never count on you to spend time with us.For a while, Avery said nothing. They'll be thrilled with the news, she told herself. But she also understood that plans seldom went as well as hoped.Her mother was really insistent, and she didn't feel like challenging her father to a staring contest.With a deep sigh, she let out her frustration. "It's cool, Mom. In an hour, I'll give you a call.Mrs. Blanc responded, "But you're phoning now."She fabricated an emergency, saying that "something came up."She needed some time to get her act together if they were going to transition to video. As a result, she would need to prepare herself mentally for the probable consequences.Avery drummed her pen on the desk as she thought out the perfect opening line for her speech. She presented the evidence, considered potential drawbacks, and devised responses to her father's possible objections.Every passing minute was like a second, and she used that time to psych herself up even more.Tristan didn't know how to interpret Avery's actions since he'd never seen her behave this way before. She was irrationally agitated, pacing in front of her desk and mumbling to herself."Avery?" After placing the order on her desk, Tristan inquired. Is there anything wrong?Suddenly, she stopped, turned around, and looked at him. Yes, of course, why wouldn't it be? And what's with all the food you keep giving me?After that, he let out a sly chuckle. He smiled and replied, "It calms you down."She rolled her eyes, but she devoured the muffin none the less. Oh, my, he was so correct.She considered herself a multifaceted individual, but when her emotions were running high, nothing could soothe them like her favourite comfort foods.Are you going to explain to me why you keep arguing with yourself and pacing back and forth all the time? Tristan crossed his fingers at her desk. I'm here if you want to vent about anything that's upsetting you.Avery laughed sarcastically as she brushed crumbs off her shirt. "You know, Tristan, borders aren't only there so we can distinguish between countries."Sorry to interrupt. with a puzzled expression on his face, he questioned."How am I going to have any alone time to ponder with you and my mom around?"The speaker stammered, "Uh... your mother? What's-"She shook her head, saying, "Just- forget it."Essentially, she had overextended her welcome. This entire business with confronting her dad... She was being thrown off by it.He got to his feet and apologised to Miss Blanc, saying, "Miss Blanc, I didn't want to insult you." "You seemed to be in need of-"Avery stood firmly with her arms at her sides. If I need your assistance, I will definitely ask for it. For the love of God, don't pry into my life until you hear me say, "Tristan, I need your aid."It goes without saying. He murmured an apology and started to go.She yelled after him, "And shut the door behind you." In a minute, I have to go for a crucial meeting.Her mouth had no time to cool down her remarks before the phone rang. Time was a concern, so she checked her wristwatch. The man was never late.She smoothed her hair for a second before responding.What was it that you wanted to tell us, sweetheart? The query came from Mr. Blanc.Being direct to the point as is customary.Avery huffed and straightened her shoulders. In a direct and unapologetic statement, she told her parents, "Mom, Dad, I'm pregnant."As a gasp escaped her, Mrs. Blanc smothered it, but Mr. Blanc showed no emotion. He sat there, staring at his daughter with a calculating expression on his face.Avery stared at her father, daring him to ask her any questions. It was her mother, though, who handled the most of the communicating.Asking, "Who's the dad? No one here knew you were dating. I'm dying to meet him, but when can I expect it to happen? When asked how he felt about being a part of our family, he said, "How does he feel?"“Uhm...” Avery's mask cracked momentarily, but she covered it up quickly. As for the paternity of this child, I have no idea. But that's beside the point. What Really Matters-"Avery jumped at Mr. Blanc's whack on the desk. "What the hell is wrong with you, Avery? We won't accept it if you go out and sleep with random guys all the time. I expect more from you as the successor to our kingdom than that.As in, "It's not like that!" As a result, Avery lost his temper. I refuse to have sex with a number of guys.Mr. Blanc crossed his arms over his chest and sat back in his chair. It was evident that he was quite angry about what had happened.Avery did a dad impression by crossing her arms and leaning back in her chair. She looked at him again, just as unyielding as ever.That's not how your dad meant it, honey, Mrs. Blanc reassured her son. That's all: "It's just a bit surprising. With the baby, what are your plans?Avery looked at her mom in complete disbelief. I'm going to keep it. In this case, it makes no difference who the father is. Still, it's my baby, and no matter what, I'll adore it.Mr. Blanc's repeated "Keeping it" with a terrifying chuckle. Someone could ask, "What do you think this is, a soap opera?"Well, the way you're acting,..."A questionable sound prompts the question, "What was that?"Mrs. Blanc interjected, "Stop it, you two," just before the younger Blanc's father was ready to unleash hell on her. "Shouting at each other won't help us solve this problem."Avery responded, "Listen," stifling her frustration. There will be no permission request on this call. I hope I'm not causing any trouble by telling you this, but...Mr. Blanc said, "You have two options in this situation. Either involve your spouse in your news, or terminate the pregnancy. You get to decide."Avery was about to respond angrily, but the phone was cut off before she could. She looked at her phone's blank screen, remembering her father's rage-filled gaze.Get married or get rid of it. To what extent does his mental state warrant such questions? Had he had a nervous breakdown since she last saw him?No matter how long passed, Avery still couldn't bring herself to get up from her desk, even after everyone else in the office had long since gone home. She kept hearing her father's words in her mind."I'm in such a pickle." The woman buried her face in her hands.Her stomach began to churn as if that weren't horrible enough. "Oh, God."With the help of the trash can, Avery bent forward and emptied her stomach contents.It seemed as if Tristan had been spying on her the entire time when he stormed into her office. The man knelt down next to her at her desk and placed a glass of cool water in front of her.While she coughed, he tucked her hair behind her ear and caressed her back softly. It's OK, he reassured me. In other words, "Everything will work out OK."Exhausted, she wiped her lips with the back of her palm and slumped back in her chair. "Damn the morning sickness."He raised his head and stared at her, horror evident on his face. "Good morning, what's up?"Her secretary was a very kind man. Always willing to go the extra mile to assist her. Avery suddenly had a thought as he gazed at her with that expression on his face.For once, everything were going in her favour, and the adrenaline surge caused her to sit bolt straight in her chair.Tristan, darling, precious, Tristan...Are you all OK, Miss Blanc? he inquired nervously.She felt guilty for a split second, but the feeling quickly passed. It was her father's insistence that she go through with this. She had been trapped by his decision.I'm going to need your assistance, and you know I've promised to come to you in the past when I've said that.He backed away from her, clearly embarrassed by his intrusion into her workplace. Simply by being in such close proximity to her. Contacting her...He murmured gently, "I remember," and he didn't take his gaze off of her.She exhaled and leaned forward, supporting herself on her elbows and knees. To which Tristan replied, "Well, I'm asking."

Chapter 3 - The Agreement

Can you believe it? To repeat himself for the hundredth time, Tristan inquired. I had no idea you were dating at all.Avery said, "Oh, yeah," before assisting him in standing up. "A few of months ago, I had a one-night stand."The speaker gasped, "Wh- wait, what?" His orbs of vision were enormous, bulging saucers atop his skull.She thought it rather humorous, honestly."You're staring at me like I have three heads," she joked. But individuals often engage in such behaviour, Tristan. To be an adult and have that freedom is half the joy.It's obvious that's not what I had in mind. But-”"Stop stuttering and tell me now..." Do you intend to carry it out? How about we act like we're engaged and you're carrying my baby?To express his continued shock, he shook his head gently. “Why? Why me?"Avery let out a long sigh. This is why: "I believe in you." She waited for more inquiries, but when he didn't come, she replied, "I'm keeping this kid, and in order to pacify my dear father, I'm going to need you to do something for me."Tristan sat at her desk and waited. You mean that was the subject of the prior phone call? You were talking to your dad, right?With a nod, she confirmed my interpretation. Without a spouse to speak of, he will not acknowledge my kid as the successor to Blanc Holdings. She gave him a gentle elbow poke. To which I reply, "That's where you come in."He rubbed the back of his neck and exhaled deeply.The request is not as serious as "Jesus, it's not like I'm asking you for a kidney over here."Tristan let out a snort, and the tension in his shoulders faded. It's just that..." "I know, I just..." To be honest, I didn't think-"You and I both say, "Yeah. I've always desired a family of my own, and Tristan is my last, best hope. With anticipation in her eyes, she stared at him. “So...? The question is, "What do you think?"The two of them had been sitting there in quiet for what seemed like an eternity with her query unanswered. Avery felt her luck had run out when a million thoughts flashed behind his eyes.Finally, he responded, "Okay, I'll do it."Inquiring, "You will?" She hadn't prepared for it, but she gathered herself fast. You will, I mean. "Oh my God, that's fantastic!"To which I replied, "You sound astonished," to which he chuckled.When asked, "How come?" I pause and say, "I don't know. That's okay, I was surprised by your affirmative response.She turned back to Tristan, still in awe that he would risk everything for her.He smiled at her and extended his hand. She let herself be pulled to her feet when she momentarily gave in and put her hand in his.Thanks a lot, I really don't know what I'd do without you.Tristan abruptly moved and slammed Avery against the desk, silencing her. He put his hands on each side of her, leaving just a couple of inches of space between them, and held her down.You've got me stumped.He questioned her in a sly manner, "Does this mean I can behave like a true fiancé?" before rubbing his body suggestively against hers.Her lips twitched, but she couldn't find the right words to say. She appreciated his directness, not because of it.Her chest tightened, her pulse quickened, and a rush of air from her lungs. Curiously, she felt the same as she had the night she first met the stranger.Her secretary, Tristan, was arousing a strong sexual desire in her. she was certain she'd never experience again."Tristan, I- I dunno if-"He broke off from her with a grin on his face. "I was joking, so chill down."She didn't even mind that his gaze consumed her whole being. The unmistakable bulge on the front of his jeans.She knew about his puppy love the moment it began. It was endearing, and she saw no harm in it.This time, though...She pushed away from her desk and said, "It could really be a good idea for you to behave like a genuine fiancé." "Having witnesses who can corroborate our claims will provide credibility to our tale."In that case, he said, extending an arm to her. "How about I set up a date night with your future spouse so we can talk about this?"When he extended his arm, Avery smiled and grabbed it. Naturally, sweetie. We have to make sure we don't mess up the next interrogation.***Avery felt much worse the next day than she had the night before. Tristan showed there promptly at 10 a.m., and he was immediately able to gauge her mood.He made himself at home in the kitchen and suggested, "How about I make you up some breakfast?"You are under no obligation to act in that manner.“Nonsense. It'll put you in a better mood.She sat at the kitchen counter, where he entertained her with stories and jokes as he worked his culinary magic. It was far more than she had anticipated, and it accomplished its intended purpose: making her feel better about having him around.Between bites of scrambled eggs, Avery gushed, "You're very wonderful chef."A shrug from Tristan, and he sipped his coffee. A bachelor's education is invaluable.When asked, "Why are you still single? Like, you're attractive, you're successful in your career, etc. You must have a swarm of fangirls following your every move.Once she realised the intimate nature of her inquiry, she quickly turned away from him and back to her food. They may have been "fake engaged," but that didn't provide her any insight into his private life.But

Tristan, to to her astonishment, didn't see it that way.He finally said, "I've been waiting for the ideal lady to steal my heart." This prompts me to say, "Which reminds me-"She glanced up just in time to see him take a little black box from his pocket."What are you doing, Tristan?"Since we are now engaged, I wanted to give you this.He slid open the jewel case and saw a stunning ring. Avery's size was just right for the ring, which was made of rose gold and included a single round ruby.Rubys are her absolute favourite gemstone, she said.The man was satisfied with his accomplishments and leaned back in his chair. "What, you don't say?"***As they approached her parents' home, Avery saw that the porch was already set up for afternoon tea. Mr. and Mrs. Blanc are sitting at the table in the bright morning light, with all the trimmings.She murmured a mumbled "Oh God" beneath her breath.Tristan stepped out to open the door and reassured her, "You've got this."On the porch, she introduced Tristan Hayes to her parents. A.K.A. "My fiance and the future father of my kid."“Hayes... In reference to Hayes, Inc., I assume. Asked Mrs. Blanc."No, ma'am." I wasn't that fortunate. Tristan said, "I'm simply a regular man who happens to work with your daughter."He accepted her offered hand and gave it a firm shake. Mr. Blanc didn't move at all, and Tristan shifted his weight awkwardly from one foot to the other.You lied to us when you stated you didn't know who the father was. Mr. Blanc's eyes furrowed as he scrutinised the two of them.Avery sat forward and gave him a bold look into her eyes. Tristan saw that she was tense, so he put his hand on her back. Her body froze at his touch, but she swiftly hid her surprise by taking his hand in hers and sat down.She straightened up and stared her dad in the eye. "You're right, I did lie. You wouldn't accept it if you found out I was engaged to my secretary, so I didn't tell you."I have my doubts." Even while he spoke to Avery, he maintained a steady gaze on the guy at her side.Greetings, Mr. Blanc-""Don't Mr. Blanc me," her father pleaded. Say you know she didn't make you do this only to avoid having to find a new home for that youngster. If you want to tell me anything, you need to look me in the eye.There was a noticeable stiffening on Avery's part next to Tristan, but the latter remained remarkably composed. A soothing embrace preceded his words to her."It might look that way, sir, but that's far from the truth," he said. I'm more familiar with your daughter than you are. I know she dislikes meeting you like this because you frighten her." Tristan moved forward and his arrogance climbed to the same level as Mr. Blanc's.Sorry to interrupt.Mrs. Blanc put her hand on her husband's shoulder to help him remain calm. We urge you to take it easy.However, Tristan wasn't through yet.The tea you provide makes her feel sick, therefore she despises it. She really like the muffins, but I know she has a preference for the shortbread over the chocolate chip cookies.Mr. Blanc relaxed in his chair, and Avery could see that he was both astonished and pleasantly pleased by Tristan's bravery. He appreciated it since no one had ever confronted him in such a way before.Great as that is, it doesn't change the fact that you can't have Mrs. Blanc's kid, she remarked. This is frowned upon in the social circles we frequent since you are not of the same social standing.Avery's temper flared and she pounded her fist on the desk. His social standing is of no consequence to me, and it shouldn't be to you either. He's the father of your future grandchild and he genuinely likes me. Things like that are important to me, and they should be to you as well.She was confused as to her motivation, but the effect of Tristan's admiring stare on her was pleasant nonetheless. To her relief, she had an opportunity to defend him for a change.After all these years of his being there whenever she needed him, it was the least she could do.Softly saying, "Avery, please don't create a scene," Mrs. Blanc asked Avery to calm down.Whether you like it or not, Avery said, "You wanted a man in the picture, and the man of my choice is Tristan. I'm not going to hear another argument against him staying.Avery and Tristan departed in victory, but as they approached her vehicle, her strong front began to waver. She understood the implications of using such tone with her parents, therefore she never did. But in the end, she was satisfied since she had accomplished her goal.At that, Tristan swivelled around to face her. Considering that we are engaged, it may be a good idea for the two of us to start living together. Are you willing to consider the possibility?

Chapter 4 - Moving In Together

Are we done with this now?" As Tristan entered Avery's apartment carrying a hefty package, Avery questioned him.As he kicked the door shut, he exclaimed, "Yeah, that's it."Then he set the box down and took a glass figurine of two young boys from his pocket.I only need a spot for this little guy," he replied, pointing at it.What is that? Avery approached him for a better look.When I first moved out of my parents' home, my closest friend gave me this as a present.When he gave her the figurine, she looked at it with excitement. She made her way to a huge bookcase crammed with framed photographs and many collectibles. After giving the figure a quick once-over, she placed it on a bare shelf.There we go," she said triumphantly.As Tristan flipped through the photos, he said, "Wow." Somewhat unusual for someone like you to have so many photographs.What prompted such a statement? When he didn't immediately respond to her question, she felt awkward. Clearly, I understand. It's because in your mind I'm a soulless machine that can't imagine doing anything except working. To tell you the truth, I'm simply the kind of person that doesn't like talking about myself in public.She spun around and left before he could complete his sentence.However, he smiled at her response since he knew he was lucky to be let into her world. He looked at the objects next to the pictures and tried to deduce their meaning. He took up the dead rose from next to her mother's photo and spun it in his fingers.Avery stepped up to him and said, "Please be cautious with it." "I don't want it to be destroyed since it's unique."Avery carefully removed the rose from his hand and replaced it on its stand. As her fingers traced the picture frame, her eyes took on a wistful expression, and she sighed, but then she was back to her regular icy self.What are these things?" Tristan inquired, his gaze wandering across the bookcase.With an infectious gleam on her face, Avery told him, "These are the artefacts I collected to remind me and my family of the happiest times of our life." The rose, for instance, is part of the original bouquet my dad gave my mom on their first date. When my parents adopted Victorine, the first thing I did was give her the teddy bear.Avery approached the stuffed animal. She looked down at it lovingly while holding it in her hands and giving it a soft squeeze. She set down the bear once again and made her way to a portrait of two young women.Avery stroked the golden chain between her fingers and said, "This is my share of the best friends forever necklace I ordered." The remaining half belongs to Laurel. She has worn it nonstop since I gave it to her fifteen years ago, during the whole of our lasting relationship.Avery set the necklace back down with a chuckle and moved to a shelf where there was a frame but no image. There was no image, just a quote:Remember your adversaries, because it is they that build your character.A ring box containing a stunning diamond ring was displayed in front of the quotation. Avery closed the box with a clap, her glee evident as she stepped away from the rack.Tristan was confused, but she sat down on the sofa as if nothing had occurred.He gave the exhibit one more glance and concluded that her loved ones were very important to her. Her cherished photographs and other mementos ran counter to the image she gave him.She didn't seem to be as distant as he had assumed, which made him question if many of his assumptions were incorrect.Is it a ring for a proposal? As he sat down across from her, Tristan inquired."Yeah... That hapless sod. Avery smiled as she rose to her feet and headed for her room. A late hour has come. We need to get some sleep.Avery's wariness of Tristan persisted, and she made no effort to get too close to him. She found herself becoming more comfortable with him and admitting her feelings as their time together progressed.Since his influence on her was unsettling, she decided it was prudent to maintain a safe distance.Tristan was taken aback by Avery's response to his query. He was troubled by the fact that she was laughing off her distress.As he paced in front of her closed bedroom door, he mentally formulated a plan to finally approach her. When he pressed her for details, he was interrupted by the sound of her vomiting.Without thinking twice, he opened the door to her room and saw her sobbing on the toilet.Hello, how are you doing? In front of her, he knelt down.He attempted to comfort her by running his fingers through her hair.She looked up at him with teary eyes and then, to his amazement, she chuckled. To which the recipient responds, "Oh my God, have a look at me."Taking a deep breath, he could see disappointment in her eyes. After all, I am a badass, right?Even tough guys experience morning sickness, he said.Yep, well, Avery struggled to get to her feet. I can't afford to show any signs of weakness right now.She became disoriented at an inopportune moment, and Tristan quickly sprang to catch her. He swooped down and scooped her up in his powerful arms, carrying her to her bed before she could say a word.She spoke the word "boundaries," but her voice sounded more weary than threatening.The speaker sighed and said, "Yes, yeah, whatever." He took her by the hand and led her to her room, where he set her down on the bed tenderly. "Chill out for a while."She murmured, "I don't need anybody." Furthermore, "you have no right to direct my actions."However, even with that, it was obvious that she had lost all will to fight.Her openness moved him to his very core, and he felt a tremor in his resolve. He felt compelled to remain at her side and shield her from any danger.Then, his infatuation blossomed into something more, and he found himself wishing for things he hadn't given much thought to before.Avery watched Tristan gently take off her heels with a combination of delight and uncertainty on her face.Up her body he worked, taking off anything he judged superfluous. When he was done, he went to her bedroom closet to choose something more relaxing for her to wear.While Avery changed, Tristan poured her some tea and a cold compress. He stripped down to his underwear and returned to Avery's room.He brought her the tea after she was in bed, and he was reluctant to leave again.When he sat down next to her, she abruptly turned around to look at him. Tristan stroked the cool compress over her forehead and she closed her eyes in absolute joy. Her reply excited him emotionally and physically, so he ran the towel over her whole face and neck."Are you feeling a bit better now?" Tristan inquired, prompting him to get to his feet.Avery grabbed his shirt and dragged him back to the ground. You don't have to go through all this trouble. We're simply playing a game; I'm pregnant, not dying.The message in her eyes contradicted what she was saying, shattering him to his very core. Even if he wanted to, he couldn't ignore her hushed pleadings.He agreed and sat down beside her. This charade we're engaging in doesn't imply I don't care about you, however. Whether you're sick, lonely, or simply want some quiet time to yourself, I'll be here.He was taken aback when Avery moved closer to him, and he found himself compelled to reach out and touch her.Avery's sense of exposure was unprecedented. His comments not only caught her off guard, but they also rekindled a part of her that she had long since given up hope of ever reviving. He did something for her that no one else has done since she was a teenager: he made her feel loved and valued.In addition, he provided her with solace unlike any she had ever had before. She decided to take advantage of the opportunity since it was just what she needed right then.Avery, who wounded you so badly? 'Tighten your grasp,' Tristan urged, and he did.Avery responded with irritation in her voice, "No one injured me," and she turned her back on him.Tristan stretched out his body and sighed. He couldn't fathom why Avery wouldn't confide in him, but then he remembered that he had secrets of his own.He felt it wasn't worth risking his relationship with her.I apologise. I apologise if I offended you. Simply by running his fingertips over her back, he managed to calm her down.Avery faced him once again, and her grin was warm and endearing. There's nothing wrong with me, and I'm not broken, either, so don't worry about me, Tristan. I don't want a guy to come into my life and attempt to mend things that are OK the way they are.I'm not trying to make you better. Tristan beckoned her in for an embrace and told her, "You're already flawless and anybody who attempts to alter you is a fool of epic proportions."The two made each other laugh, and Avery went back to where she had been. She soon slept off while Tristan tinkered with her hair. He debated staying, but ultimately decided to go.While Avery was sound sleeping, Tristan was transfixed by her beauty. He saw the expansion and contraction of her chest as she breathed. Her adorable grin, as if she were experiencing the most wonderful dream, formed on her lips.He whimpered like a puppy in love and said softly, "Tristan Hayes, you are the greatest moron on the earth." One would reasonably ask, "How could you be so naive as to fall in love with a lady like her?"He froze when Avery put her arm over his chest. After months of wanting to be in such close proximity to her, it was incredible to finally be there. He tried to appreciate it, but he just couldn't do it.You committed to something, and now you must see it through. Crushes and romantic interests may be quite dangerous sidetracks that cause you to lose focus. He stated it in a loud whisper, "You need to quit this obsession and concentrate on the work at hand.Avery's tighter hold effectively silenced him.***Avery and Tristan went to Blanc Holdings together the next morning.As they passed Tristan's desk, Avery said quietly, "You don't have to accompany me all the way to my office."He said innocently, "Why not?"Since word of mouth is inevitable."They already observed us arrive in the same vehicle and walking in together. If they wanted to talk they would be chattering about that."They approached her door and he put a palm close to her head, essentially shutting her in."People are staring," she mumbled as she slid from under his arm and dashed inside her office.Tristan leaned against her door for a second and he couldn't stop himself from smiling. It took him a minute to gather his bearings and he grumbled as he moved away from the door and returned to his desk."So, are you and the boss woman genuinely getting it on?" Cam inquired as she took a seat on Tristan's desk.Her audacity astonished him, and he didn't know what to reply. He went to Avery's office and saw her standing at her large glass door with her arms crossed over her chest.She was observing him, and he found it a bit unnerving.To be preoccupied with other things at the moment. He pointed to the stacks of papers that had accumulated on his desk. Find something or someone else to occupy your time. Or, better still, "do what you're supposed to be doing."Cam cocked an eyebrow at his apparent irritation but refrained from commenting on the matter. She went out of his way and let him perform his work without resisting.Tristan turned to look at Avery again, but she had already left.***After yet another meeting, Avery was making her way back to her office when she overheard some of the female coworkers laughing it up in the break room.Do you believe there's anything more between Tristan and Avery? one of the females inquired.The answer is probably not. "Avery doesn't do relationships," meaning that she doesn't engage in them. I've lived here for four years and I've never seen a single man. I mean, not even one! So if Tristan believes he has a chance, she said, "he's making a terrible mistake."Maybe he doesn't have a chance with her, but he has a good one with me. "I've had a crush on him ever since he began working here, and I believe it's time for me to make a move," the first female remarked.Avery's ears perked up at her sharp words, and she stormed off, baffled as to her source of ire. Neither she nor Tristan were seriously dating. She wouldn't have wanted that, anyhow.I'm simply annoyed that they're getting in the way of his productivity. She persuaded herself, "That's all I need.Avery resolved to take care of the problem once and for all, so she convened a meeting of the employees.In light of the recent gossip about my private life, I feel it necessary to remind everyone here that we are at work. Your business in my private life is none of your business, and vice versa. No, this is not a barbershop, and I will not put up with your antics.The argument Avery was making was obvious, and it seemed that everyone had heard and understood it.You can come talk to me directly if you have any inquiries. That way, at least, the truth will be revealed to you.We will have a disciplinary meeting if I catch any of you slacking off or causing problems for your coworkers because of this. Take my word for it; you won't be pleased with the results.Avery walked out of the meeting room confident.She was certain that her threat would cease the rumours and discourage the females from talking to Tristan. She was headed to the workplace when she suddenly felt sick to her stomach.She ran into the nearest public restroom and vomited. She remained in her cube after wiping her mouth because she heard two ladies entering the building.There's no doubt that she's fucking him. One said, to Avery's chagrin, "It was clear from the meeting and the fact that he was getting special treatment."That's evident why his employer is still employing him. Nobody other has lasted this long, so it must imply he's making her happy in more ways than one.The impulse to smack one of them was making Avery's hand twitch, but then she had a better one.

Chapter 5 - A Spark

As Avery emerged from her cube, the females froze in shock. Aiming to alleviate her nausea, she turned to face them after splashing cold water on her face and chest.Each of the four females exchanged glances, but no words were said.With that, Avery walked toward the entrance.She knew they had no clue what they were getting themselves into when they followed her. She dragged Tristan by the shoulder and brought them to his desk.Tristan raised his head and caught a glimpse of the four ladies standing behind her. In an instant, he swivelled in his seat and went to the side.As she sat on his desk, Avery's tight skirt cinched up around her toned legs. She crossed one leg over the other and curled her fingers around her knee, which caused the skirt to rise slightly.She loomed over the other women by leaning forward and staring them down.Tristan took a deep breath as his gaze lingered on Avery, who was every bit the attractive boss. To him, the manner she was sitting was an immediate hard on.Her behaviour made him want to crash into her from behind, bending her over his desk. All else faded away in the face of her dazzling beauty.What is the current marketing department project? Avery remarked, "Ashley, you work in marketing, so you should know," and everyone in the workplace heard his words.Colleagues swarmed Tristan's desk and made no attempt to disguise the fact that they were listening in. Avery wanted to break into a grin as her plan came together, but she maintained her stone face."Uhm... Ashley averted her look and answered, "I don't know anything about the project."With a nod, Avery agreed. The financial crisis? "Jennifer, you need to be aware of it."I don't know about the financial situation, Jennifer likewise avoided eye contact and murmured.Tristan put his palm to his lips as though to stifle the grin that was bursting out of it. He didn't know what had occurred to set Avery off, but he was enjoying the fact that she was humiliating the female students.She didn't always go all out like this, but when she did, it was a big deal.After being humiliated in front of others, nobody would mess with her again, no matter how much effort was put in to achieve that level of public disgrace. But when she got there, she'd give it all she had. It was one of the things that made her so fascinating and terrifying.How excited are you for the next advertising push? Is it Nately or Rebecca?Nately responded, "No clue, ma'am," while nervously adjusting her blouse.Rebecca looked down at the floor and said, "I don't know anything about the campaign."“Tristan?” Avery inquired as her eyes captivated him.He swivelled around in his chair and smiled at her."We've just about wrapped up the promotion for the new fragrance, and it's set to be released on the market next Wednesday. It's been a week since the problem in the accounting division was fixed. Moreover, we have expanded our advertising campaign for our five new scents to include television commercials."Ladies and gentlemen, give the guy who is presumably retaining his job by fucking me a hand," Avery urged.Since Tristan genuinely performs his work instead of wasting time with idle chatter, he has been able to hold his employment for as long as he has. Take it as a warning to put in a little more effort and cut down on the chitchat.Avery stood up to adjust her skirt and then faced Tristan. He had a wide grin on his face, and Avery's eyebrows shot up at his somewhat childish antics.Seeing that Avery was going to inquire, Tristan quickly retrieved the necessary documents for her next meeting and delivered them to her. He was anticipating her next move again again, and this time she couldn't help but be impressed.She responded, "Thank you," then swallowed a few times to collect her thoughts. Please notify Human Resources and have them schedule a disciplinary meeting to address the poor performance of these female employees.Avery walked up to Tristan and gave him a little tap on the back with her papers before heading inside her office.Thoughts of Tristan kept her from concentrating on her task.She glanced over at his desk and saw that he was totally absorbed in what he was doing there. She kept staring at him helplessly. The way his chiselled jaw tensed and he chewed his pen while thinking...When the delivery came with two large parcels, he was yanked out of that delightful position. Although Avery was first annoyed by the interruption, her displeasure quickly subsided.When he scooped up both boxes and carried them to her office, a breeze blew through her wide lips due to the rippling of his biceps.She pictured what he would look like shirtless and her pussy fluids poured between her legs.Express shipping. Tristan sat down at her desk with the boxes on it.Avery's attention was riveted as she studied the muscles of his chest and the outline of his abs that poked out from under his shirt.She wondered whether her craziness may be attributed to her pregnancy. How could it happen, anyway?There was, however, one thing she couldn't deny: her pretend fiancé was stunning.Hello, lovely. So, how are you doing? He inquired, drawing her seat closer.Avery forced down some water, but her cravings persisted. Saying, "Thanks, but I'm OK. I'm just a little bit irritated over the incident that occurred earlier."To paraphrase, "That was so fucking hot." Tristan tossed his head back, closed his eyes, and ran his fingers up his chest. My fiancee is both physically and mentally intimidating, and I couldn't be happier.Is it a flirtatious remark? Trying to hide the fact that she felt hot and uncomfortable, Avery softly slapped his knee.Tristan shrugged and smiled at her with an intensity that threatened to melt her underwear.He caught her hand as she retracted it and held it on his thigh. He drew her chair further closer and positioned her between his knees.She was so engrossed in the moment that she failed to see that her hand was creeping up his leg. She was so focused on looking up at him that she didn't even notice she was biting her lip.No detail eluded him, however. Tristan bent down and brushed her hair out of the way, increasing the tension between them.Tristan's whisper, "The fresh samples just came," sent a shiver of excitement down her spine. "Can I wait here while you give them a shot?"The rapid beating of Avery's heart made it difficult for her to take a deep breath. Unfortunately, I don't believe I'm able to deal with it right now. You know, why don't we give them a shot later? "When my hormones aren't making me crazy."Do you feel like you're getting ill again? Tristan glanced down at her worriedly as he cupped his hands over her face.Avery swallowed and cleared her throat as she fought the temptation to scream. Just a little bit flustered, as they say.After Tristan picked up the sample boxes, he brought Avery a glass of ice water.I'll simply store them away for the time being. He gave her a knowing wink and left her office without a word, but she watched his every step.Let me assist you with that," Samantha hurried up to him enthusiastically.Before he could say anything, she grabbed the package, which somewhat angered him. Since the beginning, Tristan had realised that she was flirting with him and he had made every effort to gently decline her advances. Unfortunately for him, she didn't seem to be grasping his argument.Each rejection just made her want to succeed even more. Though first funny, the situation soon became tiresome to him. Now that he had a shot with Avery, he wasn't going to waste it by being a doormat to Samantha.I'm going out with several of the ladies for drinks tonight and I was hoping you could come along. Upon asking, Samantha rubbed up against him."I'm afraid I can't." Tristan wasn't even making an effort to be courteous at that point.Upon arriving in the storage room, he let them in. He entered, set the box down on the display shelf, and then took the one Samantha was carrying."Oh, no!" As the door slammed shut, Samantha said.Immediately, Tristan sprinted to the door and twisted the handle.It's locked," he turned to Samantha and remarked.

www.ingramcontent.com/pod-product-compliance
Lightning Source LLC
LaVergne TN
LVHW052106160826
845678LV00015B/3398